MANNY'S MOOD CLOUDS

A Story about Moods and Mood Disorders

Lourdes Ubidia

Guide for Adults by Aimee Daramus
Illustrated by Lourdes Ubidia

Jessica Kingsley Publishers
London and Philadelphia

First published in Great Britain in 2023 by Jessica Kingsley Publishers
An imprint of Hodder & Stoughton Ltd
An Hachette Company

1

A CIP catalogue record for this title is available from the
British Library and the Library of Congress

ISBN 978 1 83997 495 3
eISBN 978 1 83997 496 0

Printed and bound in China by Leo Paper Products Ltd

Jessica Kingsley Publishers' policy is to use papers that are natural,
renewable and recyclable products and made from wood grown
in sustainable forests. The logging and manufacturing processes
are expected to conform to the environmental regulations of
the country of origin.

Jessica Kingsley Publishers
Carmelite House
50 Victoria Embankment
London EC4Y 0DZ

www.jkp.com

To the nuggets in my life.
To my family and their endless support.
To my friends who love me.

My big brother Manny has been different lately.

No, not different in how he looks,

or feels,

or sounds. Just different in how he acts.

Not to mention,
I see these clouds above his head
all the time now. I don't remember
when they first showed up.

Mom says, "Well, Elijah, we can all have little clouds above us sometimes."

"Like when we're really sad, grumpy, or happy."

Manny's clouds are different though. They're bigger and never really go away.

When Manny is angry, he has a red,
rippling cloud that roars with thunder
and lightning. He says he feels most
frustrated when his cloud is red.

When he's sad, his cloud is blue
and gloomy. It rains on him a lot.
Manny tells me to go away more
often when his cloud is like that.

His purple cloud means he is very panicked and scared of everything, even shadows.

His yellow cloud means he's really happy.
So happy, that he doesn't know what to do with himself.

Sometimes, I don't know when I can play with Manny.
I get scared when I see his yellow cloud turn red without warning.

Other times, I just leave him alone. His blue cloud makes him no fun anyway.

His purple cloud makes him talk about all the things that scare him.
Mom tells me not to laugh at the things he says.

I always try to make Manny's cloud stay yellow because that one is my favorite. I like seeing Manny happy.

Dad says we can't control the color of Manny's clouds, but we can try and help him work through his feelings.

When we are outside together as a family, Manny's clouds make people look at him funny and say things that aren't nice.

One day, my parents told me that Manny
is going to see someone called a therapist.

They said a therapist is like a doctor that helps people talk about their feelings and the things going on in their brain.

I asked Mom and Dad if Manny's clouds make him different.
They told me that his clouds are different from the little clouds
we all feel sometimes, but there was a reason for that.

They said that Manny has something called a mood disorder.

I did not understand what those words meant, but I didn't want to ask any more questions. Until one day…

He said that a mood disorder is like a feeling, like happiness, sadness, anger, or fear. Everyone has feelings, but Manny said having a mood disorder means...

MOOOOOOO

...it is harder for him to control his feelings, how strongly he feels them, and for how long.

Manny says that therapy is helping him gain control
over his feelings, because he gets to talk about them
out loud with someone who knows how to help.
He said that if I wanted, I could help him too.

Together we do yoga,

jump rope, blow bubbles,

and have family talk time with Dr. Joy, Manny's therapist, so we can all talk about our feelings.

Even though Manny's cloud is yellow more often now, there are still days when his mood clouds frustrate him.

But now, we know ways to help Manny
feel a little better on those days.

Manny continues to go to therapy with Dr. Joy.
She teaches Manny the tools he needs to control his moods.
You can use these tools too! When you are...

you can squeeze a squishy ball!

take three deep breaths.

talk about what is making you sad.

do arts and crafts!

There are many people who have mood clouds.
Some look like Manny's and some don't.

*Regardless, even though their clouds make them different,
it doesn't change how much they love us or how much we love
them, no matter what color their clouds are today.*

THE END!

GUIDE FOR ADULTS

THANKS FOR PICKING UP *MANNY'S MOOD CLOUDS.*
It is a great first step in helping your children
understand mood disorders. There are decades of
research to show that a supportive, loving home can
change the course of a child's mental health problems,
and an unsupportive one can make those problems
worse. Just by showing your children that you love them
and that you're taking care of them, you're changing
the course of the mental illness, although therapy and
possibly medication are going to be important as well.

As the book says, everybody has moods, but some people
(like Manny) have MOOOOODS. Hard to control, hard to
understand, scary and heartbreaking to watch. These
are called mood episodes, and people who experience
mood episodes are often experiencing mood disorders.

Mood disorders include depression and bipolar disorder.
In depression, people have mood episodes that include
sadness, anger, and emotional numbness. People with
bipolar disorder experience depression, mania, and/or
hypomania. Mania is a mood episode that includes
very high energy, insomnia, impulsive behavior, and
excessive confidence. Some people with mania
experience delusions (unrealistic beliefs that seem very
real to them), but that's less common. Hypomania is
often thought of as a less extreme mania. Someone in
a hypomanic episode sleeps less than usual (maybe
2–4 hours), has a lot of energy, and is more impulsive

than usual but not completely out of control. Children
with bipolar disorder have episodes that last for days,
weeks, or months and are more likely to have "mixed
episodes" that include symptoms of both depression
and mania.

TALKING ABOUT MOODS

Children can have a hard time expressing their moods in
words. You can help by:

- using the color-coded "cloud" system in this book. Let
  your children decide which color means which mood
  for them.

- helping them talk about how they feel with simple
  words: "I feel (angry, sad, empty, hyper) and it makes
  me want to…"

- making art with them. If there are dark colors,
  themes of danger, depressed emotions, or feeling
  alone, that can be an indication of their moods. Some
  children express themselves more easily in art than
  in words. Similarly, when they're playing with dolls
  and stuffed animals, their play might reflect their
  moods.

- using their favorite shows and books: "What
  character feels the same as you today?"

HOW TO HELP

When you take children to a doctor for their mood episodes, try to take them to a specialist, like a pediatric psychologist or psychiatrist. Even the best family doctor doesn't have the same expertise in child psychology. Sometimes, depression and ADHD look surprisingly alike, for example, and some mood episodes can be caused by different medical problems.

You are an essential part of your child's care. No one has their trust like you do, so there's a lot you can do that no doctor can give them. Here are a few suggestions:

- If they'll let you, hug them and hold them for comfort. If they're overstimulated and don't want to be touched, respect them. Although it can feel like they're rejecting you, they're just trying to manage their body's reactions.

- There are some excellent child-friendly meditations and yoga online. They can help you and your other children feel more relaxed too (just like in this story, Manny's challenges meant that Elijah also needed some extra support).

- Look for a caregiver's support group online, on social media, or in your area.

USEFUL RESOURCES

- Digital Shareables on Child and Adolescent Mental Health at nimh.nih.gov

- Kids, Teens, and Mental Health at nami.org

- Young Minds at youngminds.org.uk

- Children and Young People at mentalhealth.org.uk

- Jessica Kingsley Publishers at us.jkp.com and uk.jkp.com

- Meditations for Kids at mindful.org

Aimee Daramus, PsyD, is a licensed clinical psychologist specializing in the treatment of depression, bipolar disorder, anxiety, schizophrenia, and trauma. She is the author of *Understanding Bipolar Disorder: The Essential Family Guide* and is based in Chicago, IL.

ABOUT THE AUTHOR

LOURDES UBIDIA is a New York-born illustrator and animator. She attended Fiorello H. LaGuardia High School of Music & Art and Performing Arts and graduated from The City College of New York with a BFA. Since the age of 7, she has had a passion for art that has provided a solace for her at every stage of her life. She is currently fulfilling her lifelong dream of becoming a children's book designer at Workman Publishing.

Lourdes's style is textured and family-friendly, with an emphasis on vibrant colors and round shapes and curves. She is highly influenced by Nickelodeon programming from the 90s. When she is not partaking in her craft, she can be found tending to her plants in the garden or sketching every leaf she can find. However, more times than not, she is probably re-watching one of her favorite films or TV shows to seek inspiration for her next project.

If you enjoyed *Manny's Mood Clouds*, why not check out more books from JKP?

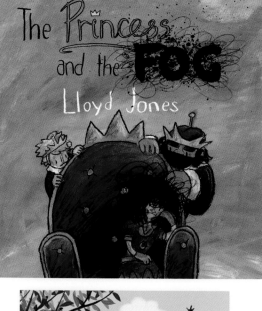

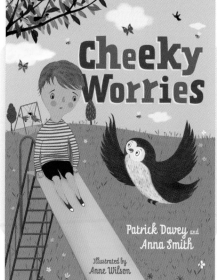